Dear Parents:

Congratulations! Your child is taking the first steps on an exciting journey. The destination? Independent reading!

STEP INTO READING® will help your child get there. The program offers five steps to reading success. Each step includes fun stories and colorful art or photographs. In addition to original fiction and books with favorite characters, there are Step into Reading Non-Fiction Readers, Phonics Readers and Boxed Sets, Sticker Readers, and Comic Readers—a complete literacy program with something to interest every child.

Learning to Read, Step by Step!

Ready to Read   Preschool–Kindergarten
• big type and easy words • rhyme and rhythm • picture clues
For children who know the alphabet and are eager to begin reading.

Reading with Help   Preschool–Grade 1
• basic vocabulary • short sentences • simple stories
For children who recognize familiar words and sound out new words with help.

Reading on Your Own   Grades 1–3
• engaging characters • easy-to-follow plots • popular topics
For children who are ready to read on their own.

Reading Paragraphs   Grades 2–3
• challenging vocabulary • short paragraphs • exciting stories
For newly independent readers who read simple sentences with confidence.

Ready for Chapters   Grades 2–4
• chapters • longer paragraphs • full-color art
For children who want to take the plunge into chapter books but still like colorful pictures.

STEP INTO READING® is designed to give every child a successful reading experience. The grade levels are only guides; children will progress through the steps at their own speed, developing confidence in their reading. The F&P Text Level on the back cover serves as another tool to help you choose the right book for your child.

Remember, a lifetime love of reading starts with a single step!

SO-BMV-942

llama llama
Anna Dewdney
dance recital fun

based on the bestselling children's book series
by Anna Dewdney

Random House 🏠 New York

Llama Llama is happy.

He is watching Luna

Giraffe practice her

dance steps.

"That was great!"

Llama Llama says.

Luna has a recital soon.

She feels nervous.

"I have a tummy ache!"

Luna says.

Llama Llama and Nelly Gnu try to help Luna.

"I know you will be great, Luna," says Llama Llama.

But Luna is still nervous.

She needs fresh air

to calm down.

Llama Llama has an idea.

"You can practice for us!"

he says.

"I'll try," says Luna.

Luna puts on some music

to practice.

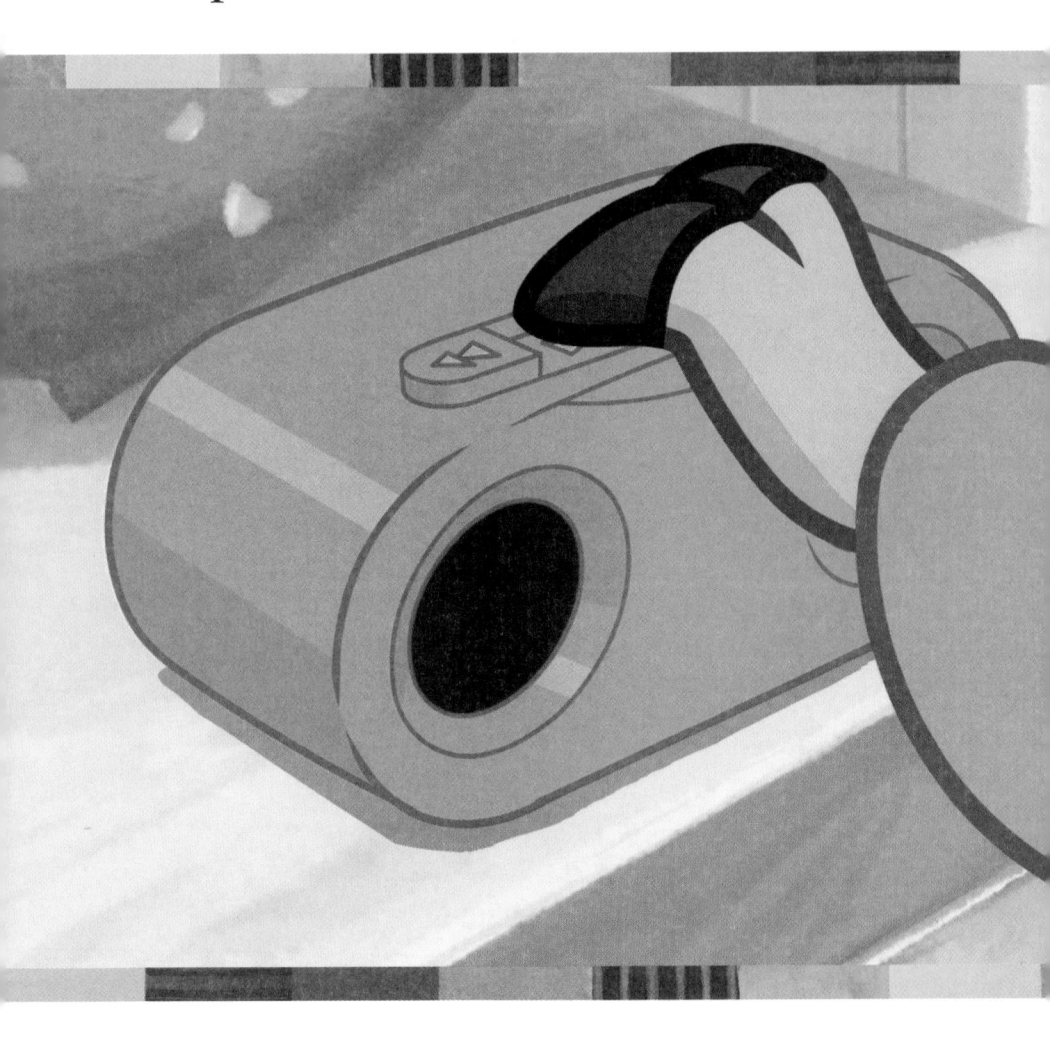

Oh no!

She still feels nervous.

Llama Llama knows how to

help Luna.

He invites her over to his house

to play.

He has a surprise for Luna.

"It's a dance machine!"

says Llama Llama.

Mama Llama tells Luna that it is just for fun.

"A few deep breaths help me feel calmer," says Mama Llama.

Luna takes some deep breaths.

Now she is calm and having fun.

"Go, Luna!" calls Nelly Gnu.

The next day, everyone gathers

for the dance recital.

"I hope Luna is not so nervous

anymore," says Llama Llama.

"You and Nelly are such good friends for trying to help her," says Mama Llama.

"I'm sure she's going to be fine," she says.

"Welcome to our dance recital!"

says Zelda Zebra.

The dancers begin to perform.

Oh no!

Luna is missing.

Llama Llama and

Nelly Gnu help look

for her.

Nelly Gnu searches the school halls.

Llama Llama searches

the classrooms.

"Luna, where are you?"

asks Llama Llama.

There she is!

Luna is outside.

Luna is still too nervous to
perform onstage.

"I can't dance with everyone
watching me," she says.

Llama Llama helps Luna.

"We're excited to see you dance,"

Llama Llama says.

Luna takes a few deep breaths.

"I'm going to try," Luna says.

"The show must go on!"

The friends race back inside.

Nelly Gnu reminds Luna
how much fun they had
on the dance machine.

"Just dance and try to have fun,"

says Llama Llama.

Llama Llama has an idea!

He brings the dance machine

to the stage.

"Put your hands together for

Luna Giraffe and Friends!"

First, Llama Llama dances

onstage.

Then more friends come up

to dance!

Now it is Luna's turn.

She takes a deep breath and

dances perfectly!

Everyone cheers.

Luna is so happy.

She is lucky to have

such great friends.

Mama Llama is proud of

Llama Llama for helping Luna.

They celebrate in the best

possible way—

with ice cream and

a dance party!